The Princess and the Packet of FROZEN Peas

For my favourite Ps, Pippa and Polly. T.W.

For my two ugly stepsisters, Sofie and Simone. S.deG.

Scholastic Press
345 Pacific Highway
Lindfield NSW 2070
An imprint of Scholastic Australia Pty Limited (ABN 11 000 614 577)
PO Box 579
Gosford NSW 2250
www.scholastic.com.au

Part of the Scholastic Group
Sydney • Auckland • New York • Toronto • London • Mexico City • New Delhi • Hong Kong • Buenos Aires • Puerto Rico

First published by Scholastic Australia in 2009.
Text copyright © Tony Wilson, 2009.
Illustrations copyright © Sue deGennaro, 2009.

National Library of Australia Cataloguing-in-Publication entry

Author: Wilson, Tony, 1972-
Title: The princess and the packet of frozen peas / Tony Wilson;
        Illustrator, Sue deGennaro.
ISBN: 9781741693362 (hbk.)
        9781741693379 (pbk.)
Target Audience: For children.
Other Authors/Contributors: DeGennaro, Sue.
Dewey Number: A823.4

Typeset in Futura, BlackJack, Linotype Tapeside and Hilde Sharpie.

Printed by Tien Wah Press, Singapore.

10 9 8 7 6 5 4 3 2 1   9 / 0 1 2 3

The Princess and the Packet of FROZEN Peas

Tony Wilson
Sue deGennaro

A Scholastic Press book from Scholastic Australia

Once upon a time

there was a **prince** called **Henrik** who wanted very much to fall in *love* and get married.

He was an **outdoorsy** type, and hoped that the *princess* he married would like hockey and camping.

There were many girls who wanted to marry a *prince*. Every time **Henrik** left the palace, groups of screaming girls would yell,

'Oh my goodness, it's him!'

and throw flowers in his general direction.

Henrik decided to ask his
brother for advice.

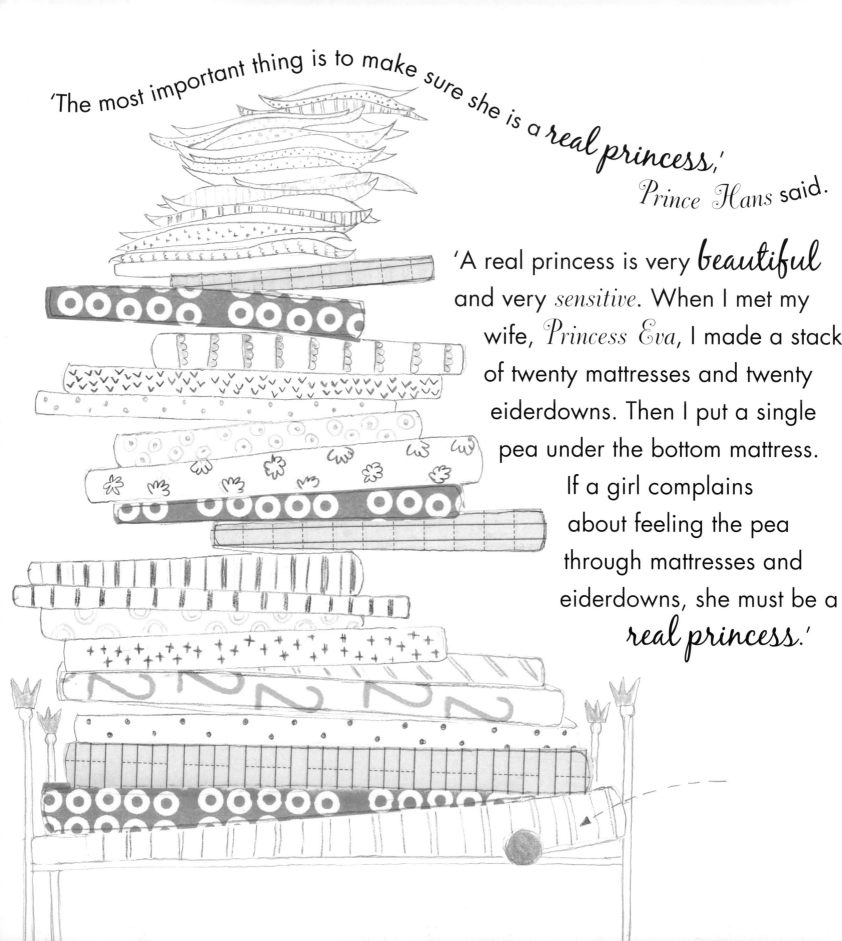

'The most important thing is to make sure she is a *real princess*,' Prince Hans said.

'A real princess is very *beautiful* and very *sensitive*. When I met my wife, *Princess Eva*, I made a stack of twenty mattresses and twenty eiderdowns. Then I put a single pea under the bottom mattress. If a girl complains about feeling the pea through mattresses and eiderdowns, she must be a *real princess*.'

'Did *Princess Eva* complain?' **Prince Henrik** asked.
'You bet—she complained a lot,' said *Prince Hans.*

Prince Henrik decided to watch *Princess Eva* to see what a **real princess** was like.

He found her at the tennis court, where she was being *sensitive* about the tennis balls.

'These tennis balls are **too bouncy**!'

He followed her to the driveway and saw her being *sensitive* about her new sports car.

'This isn't the car I wanted! I wanted one with drink holders. And yellow!'

GARAGE

Prince Henrik wondered whether perhaps
Princess Eva was a little too *sensitive*.

Prince Henrik decided he didn't want to marry a *real princess* like *Princess Eva*. He wanted to marry the exact opposite.

She didn't have to be *beautiful* or *sensitive*. She just had to like hockey and camping and have a nice smile.

And so **Prince Henrik** came up with a plan.

Whenever a *girl* came to stay,
he offered to make up the guest room.

Instead of twenty mattresses,
Henrik found one thin camping mattress.

Instead of twenty eiderdowns,
Henrik found one old sleeping bag.

And instead of a single pea,
the **prince** decided to use a whole
packet of FROZEN PEAS.

Many young girls visited, but none passed the test.

'You won't believe this.
I found PEAS in my bed.'

'I couldn't sleep at all!
There was a massive
lump under the mattress.'

'What's the deal with the
packet of FROZEN PEAS?'

1.

2.

3.

Then one morning **Henrik**'s old schoolfriend **Pippa** came to stay.

They had a great day riding horses, playing hockey and spying on *Princess Eva* as she complained about everything in the *palace*.

'If she's a *real princess*,' Henrik joked, 'I want to marry the opposite.'

Henrik and **Pippa** laughed. For the first time **Prince Henrik** noticed what a lovely laugh she had.

That night
    he decided to test her with
        the packet of FROZEN PEAS.

The following
morning
Henrik sat in
the corridor
outside the
guest room.

He waited

and waited

and waited.

Finally **Pippa** emerged, yawning.

'How did you sleep?'
asked **Henrik**.

'Fantastically well, thank you,' said **Pippa**,
handing him a packet of mushy peas.

'I found this under the mattress last night.

'It was the perfect icepack. I had a bit of a sore shin from playing hockey.'

The **prince** beamed. **Pippa** beamed back.

She had a lovely gap between her two front teeth.

'Will you marry me?' asked **Prince Henrik.**

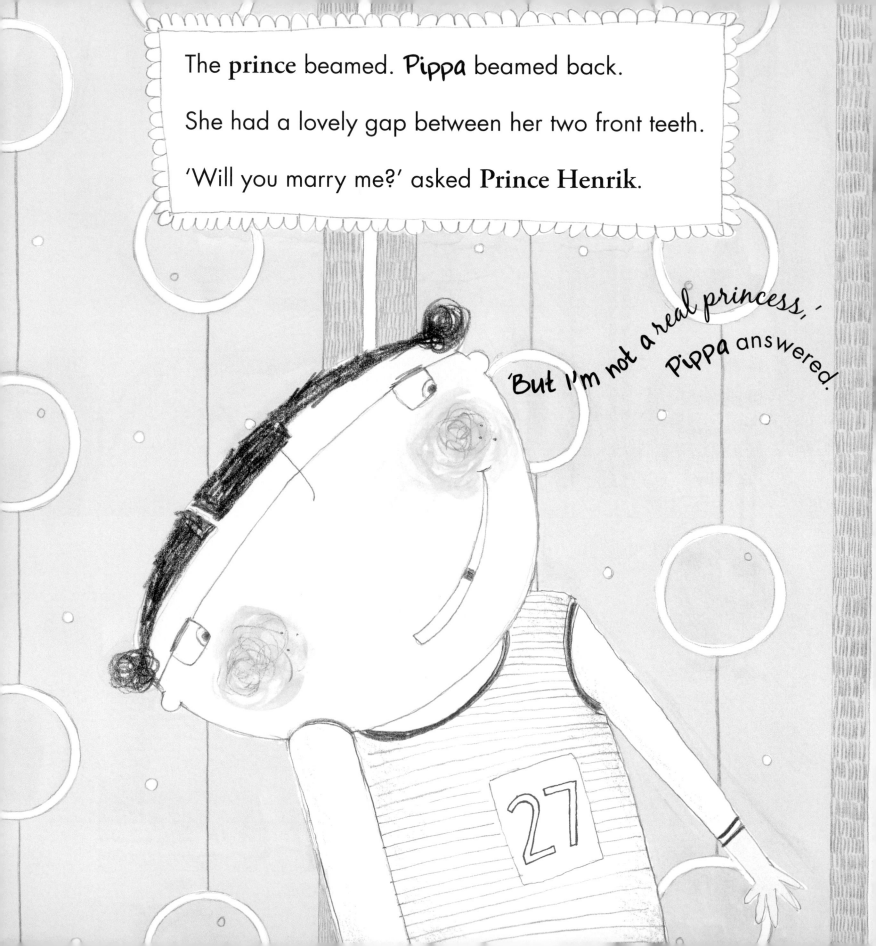

'But I'm not a real princess,' Pippa answered.

1.

2.

3.

4.

5.

6.

7.

8.